Ella & the All-Stars

by Sherry Cerino & Pam Clemente

illustrated by Nancy Cote

Ella and her sister Violet loved to practice cartwheels
in Starfish Lagoon.
"Look at me, Ella!"
"Don't swim out too deep, Violet!"
Being a big sister starfish was not easy!
As usual, Violet did not listen.

Suddenly, the waves became bigger and the sky grew dark.

"Violet, come back! A storm is coming," called Ella.

Violet glided back to the shore, but a big wave carried Ella away.

Ella tumbled faster and faster with each wave.
These were NOT the kind of cartwheels she liked to do!
A large wave scooped her up, lifted her high, and
dropped her onto a rocky beach.

"OUCH," said Ella.
"This is not MY lagoon!
The sand is rocky and the water is cold!"

An odd looking creature scurried across the rocks.
"What are you doing on MY Island?"
"Who are you?" asked Ella.
"I'm King. I rule Crab Island. You don't belong here,
you ugly fish."
"I'm lost," cried Ella.

King and the crabs pointed and chanted,

"Go away ugly fish! You are not like us. Go away!"

Ella had never met a crab before.

She wondered, "Are they all this mean and scary?"

"Leave her alone, King," said a little turtle
slowly crossing the rocks.
Ella had seen turtles in Starfish Lagoon, but none with
checkered shells.

"You stay out of this Jax," bellowed King.
 But the little turtle bravely walked through the
circle of crabs.
"I'm Ella. Will you show me the way to Starfish Lagoon?"
"I certainly will," said Jax, leading her past King and
the crabs.
 "Ella, don't be afraid of those bullies.
Swim east and soon you'll be home."

Happy to leave Crab Island, Ella swam deeper
into the ocean.
"This place is even scarier than those crabs!"
There were schools of big spotted fish and thick
slimy seaweed.

"Come here little star!"
Three big fish with teeth longer than her starfish legs
were swimming toward her!
"Oh no, Daddy warned me about sharks!"
Ella was so afraid that even her starfish legs were shaking.
Ella swam fast but the hungry sharks were faster!

"Hop on," called a little seahorse with a tiny patch over one eye.

"Hurry little star! I don't see well but I am a fast swimmer." Ella quickly hopped onto the creature's back and together they raced away from the sharks.

"I'm Davey. I come from a long line of racing seahorses."

"I'm Ella. Will you show me the way to Starfish Lagoon?"

"Swim east and don't look back, Ella. Sharks are everywhere!"

At Seahorse Crossing, Davey left Ella and raced away.

"A seahorse!

I've never seen one of THOSE in Starfish Lagoon!"

"I have to be brave and swim fast," said Ella,
but something tangled around her legs.
"Do you need help little star?"
Ella had seen lobsters in Starfish Lagoon, but this one
was different. She had only one claw!
"I'll help you," and with one snip of her single claw,
Ella was free.
"I'm Miss Shell. Swimming here isn't safe."
"I'm Ella. Will you show me the way to Starfish Lagoon?"
"You are almost there," and Miss Shell pointed the way.

Ella swam but the strong currents turned her upside down!
Nearby, a trumpet fish showed off his expert swimming skills.
"Hello, I'm Jeffery. Do you need help?"
"I'm Ella. I wish I could swim like you!"

"I can help," said Jeffery as he pointed his trumpet horn at Ella and blew as hard as he could.
"Oh myyyyy," giggled Ella as she sailed through the currents.

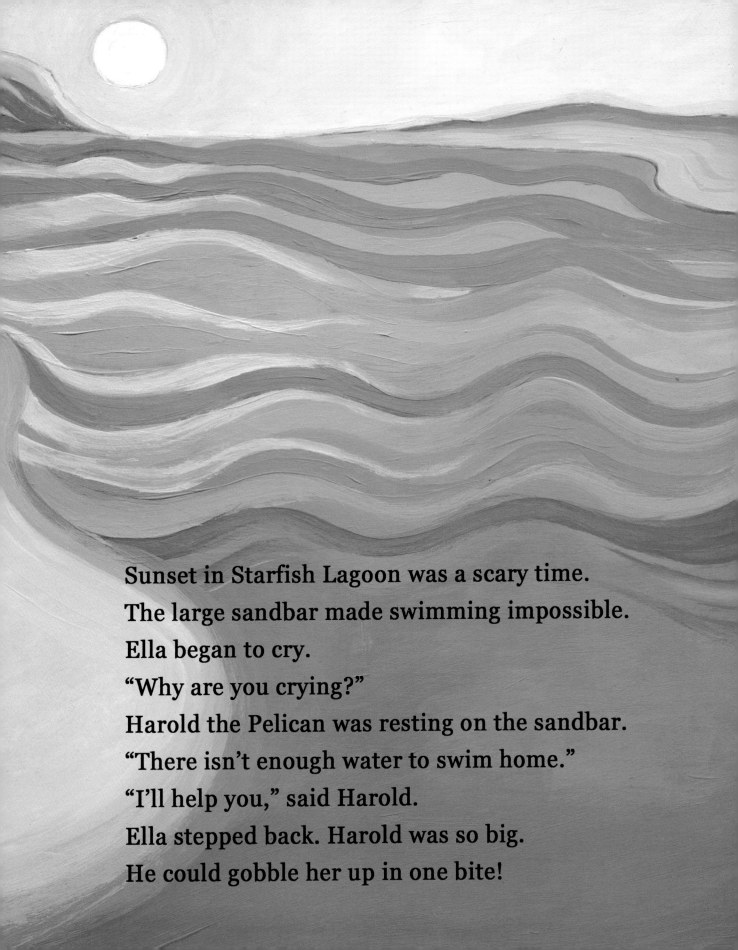

Sunset in Starfish Lagoon was a scary time.

The large sandbar made swimming impossible.

Ella began to cry.

"Why are you crying?"

Harold the Pelican was resting on the sandbar.

"There isn't enough water to swim home."

"I'll help you," said Harold.

Ella stepped back. Harold was so big.

He could gobble her up in one bite!

She looked into Harold's kind eyes and thought about Jax, the tiny checkered turtle that stood up to the bully crabs. Davey, the little seahorse who couldn't see very well, bravely raced her past the sharks. Miss Shell, the one-clawed lobster, snipped her from the fishing net. Jeffery, the odd looking fish used his trumpet to blow her through the currents. They were all so different from the fish in Starfish Lagoon, and each one had helped her. Now, she would trust Harold, too.

Together, they flew over the sandbar to Starfish Lagoon.

Harold dropped her into the warm water and Ella
cartwheeled into the arms of Violet and her parents.
Her welcome home hugs never felt better!

That night, before Ella closed her eyes she thought,
"I am such a lucky starfish to have so many friends.
They might not ALL be STARfish, but they are
ALL-STARS to me!"

Ella's new friends had become her forever friends.

To Krista, Micah, Andrea and Dan,

As children, you inspired us to be better mothers.
As adults, you inspire us to be better people.

Sherry Cerino and Pamela Clemente are sisters,
co-authors and co-founders of Ella's Way.

To Harper and Liam with all my Love. N.C.